1992

Dear Sharon's

I hope you & Tiger
can enjoy!!! these charming
cat tales

Merry Christmas Well

Susan

CAMEO CATS

THIS BOOK IS DEDICATED TO MY FRIENDS AND ALL CATS EVERYWHERE

CAMEO CATS

ILLUSTRATED BY
ISABELLE BRENT

LITTLE, BROWN AND COMPANY

BOSTON   TORONTO   LONDON

The Owl and the Pussy-cat

The Owl and the Pussy-cat went to sea
  In a beautiful pea-green boat:
They took some honey, and plenty of money
Wrapped up in a five-pound note.
The Owl looked up to the stars above,
And sang to a small guitar,
'O lovely Pussy, O Pussy, my love,
What a beautiful Pussy you are,
You are,
You are!
What a beautiful Pussy you are!'

EDWARD LEAR

The greater cats with golden eyes
  Stare out between the bars.
Deserts are there, and different skies,
And night with different stars.

VITA SACKVILLE-WEST

Cats

Those who love cats which do not even purr,
Or which are thin and tired and very old,
Bend down to them in the street and stroke their fur
And rub their ears and smooth their breast, and hold
Their paws, and gaze into their eyes of gold.

FRANCIS SCARFE

The Cat

Within that porch, across the way,
I see two naked eyes this night;
Two eyes that neither shut nor blink,
Searching my face with a green light.

But cats to me are strange, so strange
I cannot sleep if one is near;
And though I'm sure I see those eyes,
I'm not so sure a body's there!

W. H. DAVIES

Marigold

S he moved through the garden in glory, because
She had very long claws at the end of her paws.
Her back was arched, her tail was high,
A green fire glared in her vivid eye;
And all the Toms, though never so bold,
Quailed at the martial Marigold.

RICHARD GARNETT

The Cat and the Rain

Careful observers may foretell the hour
(By sure prognostics) when to dread a shower;
While rain depends, the pensive cat gives o'er
Her frolics, and pursues her tail no more.

JONATHAN SWIFT

As to Sagacity, I should say that his judgment respecting the warmest place and the softest cushion in a room is infallible, his punctuality at meal times is admirable, and his pertinacity in jumping on people's shoulders till they give him some of the best of what is going, indicates great firmness.

THOMAS HENRY HUXLEY

Mice before Milk

L at take a cat and fostre hym wel with milk
  And tendre flessch and make his couche of silk,
And lat hym seen a mouse go by the wal,
Anon he weyvith milk and flessch and al,
And every deyntee that is in that hous,
Suich appetit he hath to ete a mous.

GEOFFREY CHAUCER
From 'The Manciple's Tale'

C was Papa's gray Cat,
  Who caught a squeaky Mouse;
She pulled him by his twirly tail
All about the house.

EDWARD LEAR

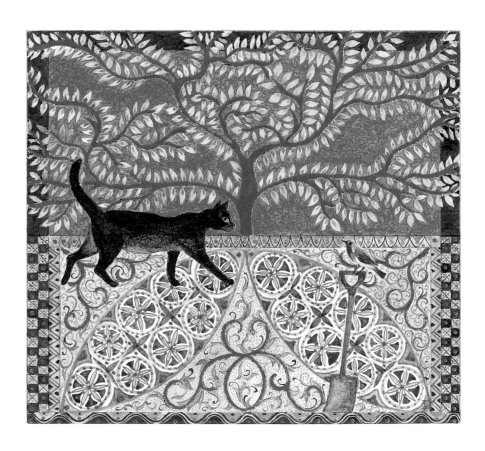

Little Robin Redbreast Sat upon a Tree

Little Robin Redbreast sat upon a tree,
Up went the Pussy-cat, and down went he,
Down came Pussy-cat, away Robin ran;
Says little Robin Redbreast: 'Catch me if you can!'

Little Robin Redbreast jumped upon a spade,
Pussy-cat jumped after him, and then he was afraid.
Little Robin chirped and sang, and what did Pussy say?
Pussy-cat said: 'Mew, mew, mew,' and Robin flew away.

From *Mother Goose*

First U.S. Edition 1992

Library of Congress Cataloging-in-Publication Data
Brent, Isabelle.
   Cameo cats/illustrated by Isabelle Brent.—1st U.S. ed.
      p.   cm.
   ISBN 0-316-10836-7
   1. Brent, Isabelle.   2. Cats in art.   I. Title.
ND3410.B74A4   1992
745.6′7′092—dc20   91-24928

10 9 8 7 6 5 4 3 2 1

First published in Great Britain in 1992 by Pavilion Books Limited

Printed in Belgium by Proost